SUMAYA SOLVES
THE SNOWY DAY PROBLEM

BY AISHA AHMED
ILLUSTRATED BY HAMNAH RIZWAN

PICTURE WINDOW BOOKS
a capstone imprint

Published by Picture Window Books, an imprint of Capstone
1710 Roe Crest Drive, North Mankato, Minnesota 56003
capstonepub.com

Copyright © 2025 by Capstone. All rights reserved. No part of this publication may be reproduced in whole or in part, or stored in a retrieval system, or transmitted in any form or by any means, electronic, mechanical, photocopying, recording, or otherwise, without written permission of the publisher.

Library of Congress Cataloging-in-Publication Data is available on the Library of Congress website.

ISBN: 9780756587970 (hardcover)
ISBN: 9780756588199 (paperback)
ISBN: 9780756588045 (ebook PDF)

Summary: Sumaya is excited to play in the snow, but before long, she's freezing! She wonders how polar animals survive the cold. Can learning more about polar animals help her stay warm on a snowy day?

Designer: Heidi Thompson

Cover artist: Loilufy

Any additional websites and resources referenced in this book are not maintained, authorized, or sponsored by Capstone. All product and company names are trademarks™ or registered® trademarks of their respective holders.

Printed and bound in the USA. 6121

TABLE OF CONTENTS

CHAPTER 1
A SNOWY DAY 7

CHAPTER 2
HOW DO POLAR ANIMALS SURVIVE? 12

CHAPTER 3
BLUBBER CLOTHES 22

HI, I'M SUMAYA!

My family moved to the United States from Somalia, a country in East Africa. I am eight years old, and I am very curious about nature and the world around me.

MY FAMILY!

SOMALI GLOSSARY

aabo (AH-boh)—dad or father

aboowe (ah-BOH-way)—brother

hooyo (HOO-yoh)—mom or mother

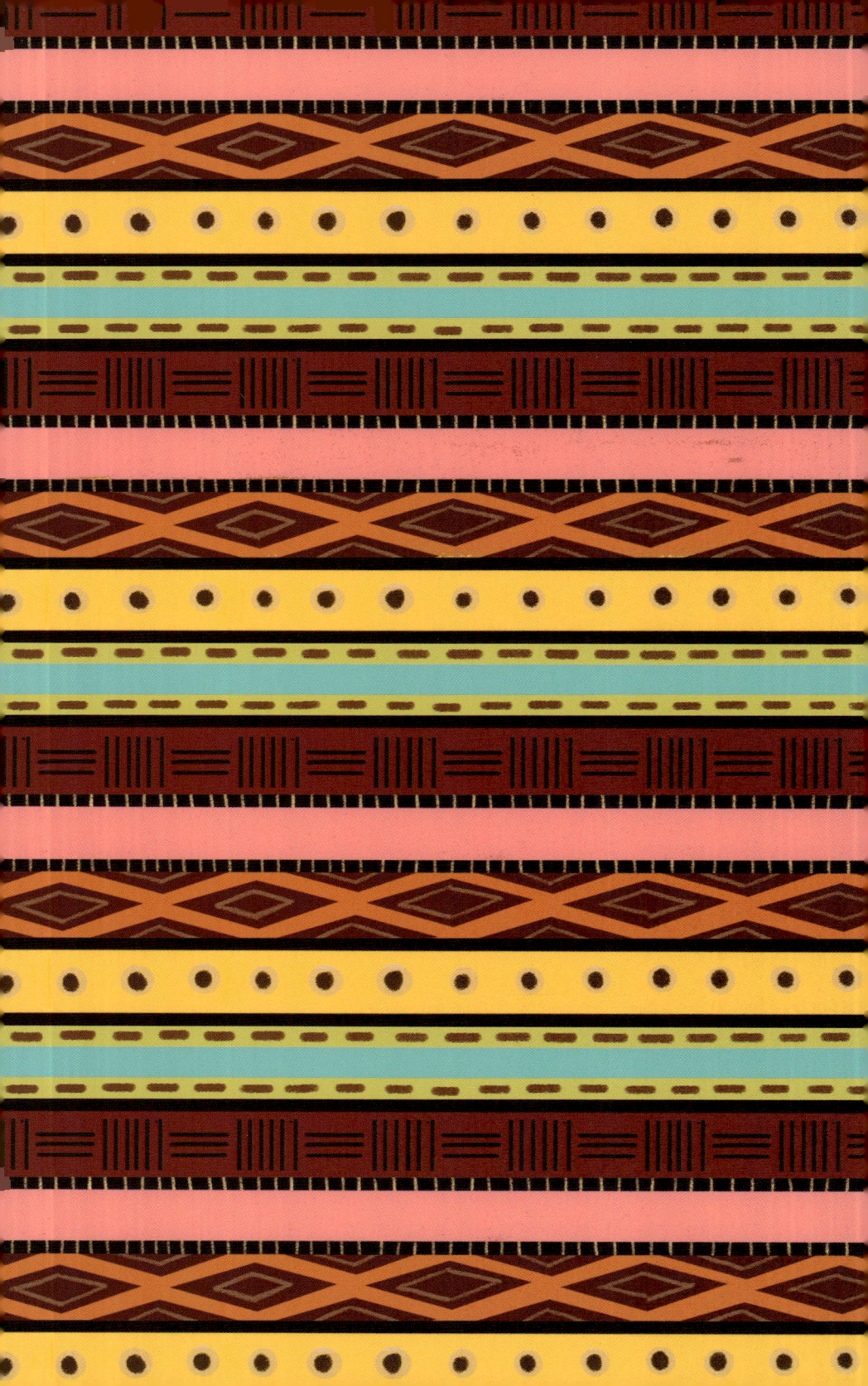

CHAPTER 1
A SNOWY DAY

"Aabo, Hooyo, aboowe, look! Look! It is snowing!" Sumaya called to her family. It was her first time seeing snow.

Sumaya's aabo, hooyo, and younger aboowe, Sahal, all looked out the window. They were amazed by the beautiful snow.

"Let's go play outside in the snow," Hooyo said.

"That's a great idea, dear! Let's go!" Aabo said.

The family put on coats and mittens and headed out the door.

Sumaya and her family made tracks through the snow. They pointed out how pretty the trees looked covered in snow.

Aabo picked up some snow. "Ah, it is sticky," he said.

Aabo made snowballs. He gently threw them at Sahal, Sumaya, and Hooyo. Soon the family was having a fun snowball fight!

"I got you!" Sumaya told Aabo as a snowball hit his shoulder.

Soon Sumaya said, "I am freezing cold!"

"I am cold too," Hooyo agreed. "Let's go inside and warm up."

Hooyo made hot cocoa. Aabo brought out the blankets. They huddled together on the couch.

CHAPTER 2

HOW DO POLAR ANIMALS SURVIVE?

"I wonder how polar animals survive the cold," Sumaya said. "They can't drink hot cocoa and cuddle under blankets on the couch!"

"Let's look it up," Aabo said.

Sumaya and her family gathered around their family computer. They searched on the internet, *"How do polar animals survive the cold?"*

Sumaya read out loud. "Polar animals, like polar bears, have thick fur and skin that keeps the heat in to help them survive the cold."

"We don't have thick fur or skin that keeps the heat in," said Sumaya.

"That's true. We do not have thick fur," said Hooyo. "But we do have thicker coats and snow pants. We should bundle up more to play in the snow."

"Let's go now!" said Sumaya. The family bundled up in thicker snow gear and headed back outside.

"I love my thick animal skin," Aabo joked.

"I am going to make a snow angel," Sumaya said. The family hurried to the backyard.

Sumaya moved her arms and legs up and down, up and down. Aabo did the same. Then Hooyo and Sahal. Angels of all sizes filled the yard.

Soon the family was cold again.

"Let's go back inside and have some more hot cocoa," Sumaya said.

"Good idea," said Aabo.

As they sipped their warm drinks, Aabo said, "We know that polar animals have thicker fur and skin that helps keep them warm. Is there anything else that helps them?"

"Let me read some more," Sumaya said. She went back to the article.

"This says some polar animals have blubber under their skin. Blubber is a special, thick layer of fat that helps animals stay warm."

Sumaya looked at her parents and asked, "Do humans grow blubber?"

"No, humans do not grow blubber," said Hooyo. "But what could you do that might help you stay warm the same way blubber helps animals?"

CHAPTER 3
BLUBBER CLOTHES

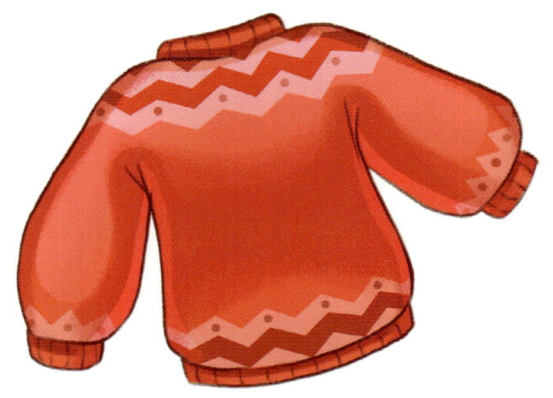

Sumaya thought about Hooyo's question. Finally, she said, "Blubber is a layer *under* animals' thick skin and fur. Maybe we need a layer under our warm snow clothes."

Sumaya put on a thick sweater. She added an extra pair of socks. Then she put all her snow gear on again.

"Let's see if my blubber clothes work!" she said, giggling. She stepped out in the snow.

"This is keeping me cozy and warm." Sumaya smiled.

"Aabo, Hooyo, Sahal, come out!" she called to her family. "Wear some blubber clothes, and let's build a snowman."

The snow kept falling while Sumaya and her family played outside.

"The snow is getting so deep," said Hooyo. "It's hard to walk through."

"I wonder how polar bears walk on snow and ice," Sumaya said. "I want to read more about polar bears. And arctic foxes, snowy owls, penguins, seals, whales, and all the polar animals!"

"Of course, Sumaya," said Aabo. "You can read more about polar animals. As soon as we have some more cocoa!"

SUMAYA SHARES MORE ABOUT POLAR ANIMALS

I love learning new things about animals. With my parents' help, I found an article on the internet about polar animals.

Here is what I learned!

1. Where do polar animals live?

Polar animals live in the world's coldest regions, like the Arctic.

2. What are some polar animals that live in the Arctic?

Polar animals that live in the Arctic include polar bears, arctic foxes, snowy owls, penguins, seals, arctic hares, narwhals, and many other amazing animals.

3. What are some things that help polar animals survive the cold?

Most polar animals have thick fur that protects them from the cold. Some animals also have an oily coating on their skin that helps hold in heat. Some also have blubber under their skin that helps keep them warm.

4. What is something that helps polar animals walk on the snow?

Polar animals like the polar bear have large feet that help them walk better on the snow. The weight of the bear is more spread out across their large feet. This makes it less likely they'll break through the top of the snow. This is similar to how snowshoes work for humans!

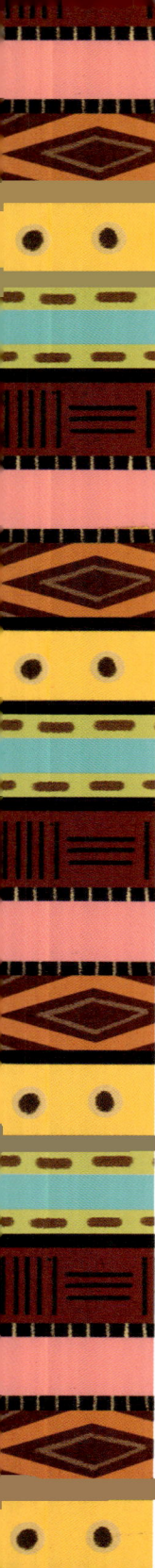

GLOSSARY

Arctic (AHRK-tik)—a region of land that is north of the Arctic Circle, around the North Pole

blubber (BLUHB-er)—a layer of special fat found in some animals, including polar bears and whales

hot cocoa (HOT KOH-koh)—a warm drink that is made by mixing a chocolate powder with hot milk or water

huddle (HUHD-l)—to crowd together

polar animal (POH-ler AN-uh-muhl)—an animal that lives in the Arctic or Antarctic

survive (ser-VIVE)—to stay alive

THINK ABOUT THE STORY

1. What did Sumaya and her family think of their first snow?

2. What did Sumaya and her family do together?

3. How did Sumaya learn about polar animals? What other ways could she have learned about polar animals?

4. How do polar animals survive the cold?

5. What could we learn from polar animals to help us better survive the cold?

ABOUT THE AUTHOR

Aisha Ahmed is a Somali American author with a background in engineering. She was born in East Africa to Somali parents and immigrated to Minnesota as a teenager. Aisha enjoys being out in nature and learning more about the natural world. Aisha also writes stories for older readers.

ABOUT THE ILLUSTRATOR

Hamnah Rizwan is a children's book illustrator from Virginia. She comes from a diverse heritage, being part Pakistani, Salvadoran, and Filipino, which has had an incredible influence on her artwork. When Hamnah isn't in her studio, you'll find her around horses, diving into epic fantasy realms like *The Lord of the Rings* (her movie-night must), or exploring the city with her family.